The Tail of the Timberwolf

by Penumbra Quill

Little, Brown and Company
New York Boston

Little, Brown and Company
Hachette Book Group
1290 Avenue of the Americas, New York, NY 10104
Visit us at lb-kids.com
mylittlepony.com

First Edition: July 2017

Little, Brown and Company is a division of Hachette Book Group, Inc. The Little, Brown name and logo are trademarks of Hachette Book Group, Inc.

The publisher is not responsible for websites (or their content) that are not owned by the publisher.

Library of Congress Control Number 2017938359

ISBNs: 978-0-316-43190-3 (pbk.), 978-0-316-43188-0 (ebook)

Printed in the United States of America

LSC-C

10 9 8 7 6 5 4 3 2 1

PROLOGUE

The moon was almost full. Though these "Cutie Mark Crusaders" and their families were proving to be an unexpected complication, The Pony kept focus on the final goal. The Livewood grew far in the distance, in a dark, shadowy patch. It was here, in the heart of the Everfree Forest, where the Artifact would be. How The Pony longed for it! Such power. Such magic!

The Artifact would be fiercely protected. Without a plan to charm the guardians of the Livewood, nopony could set hoof there. Perhaps, with the right encouragement, the guardians could be made to serve The Pony. The only way to know would be to perform a little experiment. . . .

CHAPTER ONE

"Its huge fangs were this close to my face! I could feel its horrible, raspy breath as it got closer. And closer! *Hhhhhuuh haaaaa. Hhhhhuuuh haaaaa!*" Scootaloo breathed noisily, hooves raised like claws as she stalked toward the gathered classmates in the schoolyard.

"However did you escape?" asked Pip, enthralled.

Scootaloo struck her best Rainbow Dash–cool pose. "No monster is a match for *my* wheels! I zoomed circles around that bogle! It would have eaten most of Ponyville if I hadn't chased it back into the Forest and told it to never come back—or else!"

"Uh, Scootaloo? Aren't ya forgettin' somethin'?" Apple Bloom prompted.

Scootaloo blushed. "Apple Bloom, Sweetie Belle, and Lilymoon helped, too," she added.

"And got into lots of trouble for it." Sweetie Belle sighed, remembering the whole terrifying thing. The bogle, a huge, invisible creature, had moved into Miss Cheerilee's Schoolhouse after Lilymoon, the newest student there, accidentally disturbed its nest. Against their sisters' wishes, Apple Bloom and Sweetie Belle teamed up with Scootaloo to lure the bogle back to the Everfree Forest where it belonged. With Lilymoon's help, they decorated the creature's old home with Rarity's beautiful fabric. The bogle loved it!

Most of Ponyville was impressed that

the Cutie Mark Crusaders—Sweetie Belle, Scootaloo, and Apple Bloom—had saved the town from the frightening bogle. But Rarity remained upset. "Couldn't you have used *last* season's fabrics?" Rarity had moaned to her little sister. At least their classmates thought they were heroes.

"If I ever thee another monthster," said Twist, "I'll know which ponieth to call!"

Apple Bloom scuffed a hoof on the ground and sighed in disappointment. "Maybe not. Looks like our first adventure's gonna be our last one for a while. Applejack told me not to take on any more monsters without askin' first."

"Fine by me," Sweetie Belle said. "I don't need an adventure like *that* ever again."

"That's 'cause you're a scaredy-pony," piped up Snips.

Sweetie Belle frowned at him and stomped her hoof. "I am not! I'm just as brave as any—*AAHHH!*" Sweetie Belle shot straight up, startled. Something freezing cold had touched her shoulder! She whirled to see Snails behind her, holding an ice cube with his magic. He chuckled and hoof-bumped Snips.

"You were saying?" Snips laughed. Sweetie Belle glared at the troublemakers, but before she could do anything else, Miss Cheerilee popped her head through the Schoolhouse door.

"Time for class, everypony!" she sang out. As the ponies trotted into the Schoolhouse, Sweetie Belle saw that Lilymoon was already there. She must have arrived early to avoid talking to the other ponies. Besides the CMCs, Lilymoon hadn't made too many friends yet. The violet-eyed Unicorn sat at her desk, staring straight ahead, not making eye contact with anypony.

Diamond Tiara stepped in a wide arc to dramatically avoid Lilymoon's desk. "Careful, Silver Spoon. Creepiness is catching." Diamond Tiara sneered.

Lilymoon shot them an icy look. But she gave a small smile when Sweetie Belle, Apple Bloom, and Scootaloo sat next to her. Miss Cheerilee stood in the front of the classroom, getting everypony's attention.

"Class, I hope you're excited, because Lilymoon has a special surprise for us today!"

The students all shared worried looks. Another surprise from Lilymoon was the last thing they wanted!

CHAPTER TWO

"Do you think it's another bogle?"
Featherweight whispered anxiously to Pip.
Miss Cheerilee nodded toward Lilymoon,
who placed a large bag on her desk and
glared out at the class.

"I . . . made treats for everypony," she
said awkwardly. She glanced toward the
CMCs, who gave her encouraging nods.
Sweetie Belle and her friends had told
Lilymoon that sharing sweets was a great
way to show the class she was friendly.
Sweetie Belle realized they should have
told Lilymoon to smile, too. Based on
everypony's reaction, the glaring didn't
seem to be helping.

"Isn't that nice? Let me go get plates."

Miss Cheerilee smiled, stepping outside. The students eyed Lilymoon.

"What kind of treaths?" Twist asked suspiciously. Lilymoon emptied the bag, revealing a tray of bright-green squares.

"*Ew!* What are they, frog cakes?" Diamond Tiara said, making a face.

"No!" Lilymoon protested. "They're cactus bars!"

"That doesn't sound much better," Silver Spoon said.

"You *eat* cactus?" Snails gaped.

"That'th gross," Twist said, trotting over to peer closer at the bars.

"They're a family recipe...." Lilymoon tried to explain.

"Now I *really* don't want one." Diamond Tiara sniffed. Lilymoon shot her a nasty look. Hearing a rustling noise, Lilymoon looked down to see Twist nosing around in her treat bag. Twist pulled out a large candy cane.

"I'll take thith inthead," she said, marching back to her desk.

"That's actually part of my lunch," Lilymoon protested, but Twist didn't seem to hear.

Sweetie Belle could see this was not going well. She tried to help. Loudly and enthusiastically, so the rest of the class could hear, she said, "Cactus bars sound really interesting! I'll take one!"

"I'll take two!" Apple Bloom chimed in.

"Yeah!" Scootaloo exclaimed. "They sound even cooler than lemon bars!" But when Miss Cheerilee returned with the plates, the Crusaders were the only ones who tried the green treats.

Sweetie Belle could tell Lilymoon was

upset, even though she let her blue-and-white-striped mane cover her face so nopony could see her expression. It would definitely take a lot of work to make the rest of the class accept the new student. But Sweetie Belle resolved she wouldn't give up until they did. Cutie Mark Crusaders didn't quit!

CHAPTER THREE

Lilymoon was quiet as Sweetie Belle, Apple Bloom, and Scootaloo walked her home. Sweetie Belle could see that Lilymoon was still bothered by how the other students had reacted to her cactus bars. She thought rather than bringing it up, it would be better to talk about something else. "Can you believe Snips said I'm a scaredy-pony?" she asked indignantly.

"Well, you don't really like dangerous adventures," Scootaloo pointed out.

"And yer not a big fan of Nightmare Night," Apple Bloom added. Sweetie Belle couldn't believe her friends weren't taking her side!

"I know you're brave," Lilymoon said. "You're coming to *my* house to hang out."

Sweetie Belle had to admit that Lilymoon's house was more than a little spooky. High on Horseshoe Hill, it was covered in vines, practically melting into the trees around it. The floors creaked, the shutters rattled in the wind, and Sweetie Belle could swear the portraits of the ponies on the walls were watching her when she wasn't looking. Still, friends stuck together, no matter how creepy their houses were. As the ponies approached the front door, Lilymoon's ancient aunt popped out of the front hedge, startling them all. Her eyes were wild, and her tangled gray mane stuck out in every direction.

"Auntie Eclipse... what are you

doing?" Lilymoon asked. Sweetie Belle thought she sounded worried about what the answer would be.

"Visiting my star spider friends, dear. They weave such interesting webs during the full moon, don't you think?" Auntie Eclipse held up a hoof with spiders crawling all over it. The Crusaders' eyes went wide, but they nodded politely and edged past Auntie to the front door.

"Sorry," Lilymoon whispered. "Auntie is . . . different."

"That's one word for it," Scootaloo murmured. Lilymoon led the others into her house, but before they could reach the stairs, a voice called.

"Lilymoon! You're finally home." Lilymoon's mother, Lumi Nation, walked in from the next room. She stopped when she noticed the other ponies. Sweetie Belle didn't think she was very happy to see them. "And you've brought…friends," Lumi added with no sound of welcome in her voice.

"They're helping me get caught up at school," Lilymoon said.

"Isn't that nice?" Lumi Nation said, but to Sweetie Belle, it sounded like she thought just the opposite. "Well, don't be too long. You have studying to do. And your father is counting on your help in the greenhouse. There isn't much time before tonight."

"Yes, Mother," Lilymoon said, already cantering up the stairs. The others followed, close on her hooves.

"What's tonight?" Scootaloo asked.

"And what's in the greenhouse?" Sweetie Belle wanted to know.

"And what are you studyin'?" Apple Bloom wondered. But Lilymoon shook her head.

"Upstairs," she said. Once they were safely in Lilymoon's room with the door closed, the Crusaders got some answers. "My dad has all kinds of plant experiments you can do only at night," Lilymoon explained. "And as for studying . . ." She gestured to a dusty stack of thick magical books piled up on her desk. Sweetie Belle thought they'd fit right in at Twilight's library. "My family is big on magical research."

"On top of your regular homework?" Scootaloo asked in disbelief.

Lilymoon nodded. "Guess cactus bars aren't the only weird things about us," she said with a sigh.

"They were good! And the resta the class woulda realized that if they'd tried 'em," Apple Bloom said.

"They just need to get to know you like we do," Scootaloo said.

"How? Have you seen how those other ponies look at me? They'll never forgive me for that bogle, much less talk to me," Lilymoon said.

Sweetie Belle perked up. She had an idea! "A birthday party!" she announced.

"Uh...it's not my birthday," Lilymoon said, raising an eyebrow.

"Not *yours*. Zipporwhill's!" Sweetie Belle said excitedly. "She's having a huge party tonight, and everypony is welcome! If you come, the whole class will see you playing games and having fun—"

"And realize you're just like us!" Scootaloo chimed in.

"Good thinkin', Sweetie Belle!" Apple Bloom said. The Crusaders high-hooved one another in victory. Lilymoon looked thoughtful, but before she could reply, there was a creaking noise outside her door. They all froze. Lilymoon frowned and flung the door open with her magic.

Her sister, Ambermoon, stood in the doorway!

"Were you spying on us?" Lilymoon asked. Ambermoon looked surprised to be caught but quickly covered it up with a haughty expression.

"You were stealing from me again!" Ambermoon sneered.

"I was not!" Lilymoon said, outraged.

"So somepony else keeps taking things from my room?" Ambermoon asked.

"Don't be so dramatic." Lilymoon rolled her eyes. "It was *one* candy cane for my lunch!"

"And my hoof polish and my book on dragon scales and my manebrush?" Ambermoon listed each item as if it were the most valuable treasure ever.

"I was borrowing!" Lilymoon exclaimed.

"Stealing," Ambermoon corrected.

"Better than spying," Lilymoon shot back. Ambermoon glared at her sister.

"You're not going anywhere tonight," she said, changing the subject. "Mother will *never* let you go to a Ponyville party."

"I'm not asking *Mother*," Lilymoon

said, trotting past her sister and into
the hallway. The Crusaders hurried to
follow, but Sweetie Belle looked back
to see that Ambermoon was watching
them go with narrowed eyes. Apparently,
Lilymoon and her sister didn't get along
very well.

Lilymoon led her friends outside to
the greenhouse, a small building behind
the cottage made of smoky green glass.
Sweetie Belle thought it looked like the
shiny shell of an enormous beetle squatting
on the lawn. As they all stepped inside,
Sweetie Belle could see the building was
filled from top to bottom with plants.
Some of them she recognized from
Filly Guides as dangerous. And did some
of them have ... teeth? Sweetie Belle

huddled closer to Scootaloo and Apple Bloom.

Lilymoon's father, Blue Moon, was at the back of the greenhouse. He wore goggles and a lab coat. He looked up and saw his daughter and the Crusaders. He smiled—a little too widely.

"Well, hello there!" he said through his strange grin. "What can I help you young ponies with?"

"My friends invited me to a party, and I really want to go," Lilymoon said in a rush. "It's tonight. Please say yes!"

"Tonight?" Blue Moon asked. Sweetie Belle recognized the look on his face. It was the same look Rarity had whenever she was about to say no to something. Fortunately, Sweetie Belle knew what to do. She gave Blue Moon her biggest, shiniest eyes.

"Pleeeaaase?" she squeaked. Scootaloo and Apple Bloom added their hopeful faces to Sweetie Belle's. It was too much for Blue Moon.

"All right…" he finally agreed. Lilymoon grinned to her friends. But her face froze when he added, "But only if you take Ambermoon with you."

"Don't worry, Father. I'll keep a close eye on her," Ambermoon said, stepping into the greenhouse. Sweetie Belle couldn't be sure, but she thought that sounded like a threat.

CHAPTER FOUR

Zipporwhill really does *have the best parties,* Sweetie Belle thought. All of Ponyville Park shone with light-spangled streamers and glowing balloons as the sun set. Three piñatas dangled near a table laden with every type of candy Sweetie Belle could name—and even some she couldn't.

Lilymoon hung back, a little overwhelmed, as the Crusaders led her into the park. It looked like everypony in Equestria had shown up for the birthday bash. Sweetie Belle spotted most of Miss Cheerilee's class, including Snips and Snails, who were staggering out of the park with goody bags overstuffed with candy. Sweetie Belle waved at Rarity, who was performing onstage with the Pony Tones. Nearby, colts and fillies laughed as they bounced on a pile of fluffy clouds heaped on the ground. Ambermoon was the only pony who didn't seem like she was having fun.

"I'm getting a cup of punch," she announced. "Hurry up and do your thing. We're leaving soon."

"But y'all just got here!" Apple Bloom objected. Ambermoon ignored her and trotted off.

"My sister always gets weird around the full moon," Lilymoon explained, then added, "well, weird*er*."

"SweetieBelleScootalooAppleBloom!"

an energetic Pegasus in glasses and a tiara called as she zoomed over to greet them.

"Zipporwhill! Happy birthday!" the Crusaders exclaimed in unison.

"I'm so glad you made it to my party! Who is this?" Zipporwhill asked, smiling at Lilymoon. The Unicorn backed up a little, unsure what to do.

"This is Lilymoon," Sweetie Belle said, nudging her nervous friend forward. "She's new to Ponyville."

"Hi," Lilymoon said quietly. She was startled when Zipporwhill threw her hooves around her in a fast hug.

"Welcome to my party! Have fun, okay? Don't forget to get your face painted!" Zipporwhill exclaimed happily, then flew off.

"See? Yer fittin' in already." Apple Bloom smiled at Lilymoon.

"Birthday cake *comin' through!*" a loud voice announced. Sweetie Belle looked over to see Pinkie Pie bouncing through the crowd, pushing a cart with a massive three-tiered rainbow-swirl cake with glitter sprinkles. Next to it was a smaller peanut-butter cake in the shape of a bone. Gummy Snap, also on the cart, opened his jaws to take a bite, but Pinkie stopped him just in time. "Don't be silly, Gummy. *That* cake's not for alligators. It's for Zipporwhill's puppy!"

Gummy licked his eyeball thoughtfully. The CMCs hurried after Pinkie Pie as she bounced through the crowd. Then suddenly, the pink pony looked up at the sky and stopped, frozen in place. Sweetie Belle almost crashed right into her as Gummy slid off the cart.

"Pinkie Pie? Are you okay?" Sweetie Belle asked.

"*Oh my gosh!* Do you see how big the *moon* is?!" Pinkie said, shoving the cake-serving tools into the hooves of the surprised Cutie Mark Crusaders. "Can you take care of the cake for me? I just have to do one *liiiiittle* thing. Okaythanksbye!" And Pinkie zipped off at top speed, leaving a dust cloud.

"Is she always like that?" Lilymoon asked, raising an eyebrow. Scootaloo, Sweetie Belle, and Apple Bloom shared a look.

"Yep. Pretty much. Uh-huh," the Crusaders all responded. They began cutting the cake and passing it out to the other partygoers. Everypony was having a blast until...

"*HELP! HELLLLLP!*" Shouts came from across the park. The Pony Tones stopped singing, and everypony turned to see Snails and Snips come racing into the party. They looked terrified. "It's… after…us!" Snails gasped, trying to catch his breath.

"What? What is after you?" asked Zipporwhill, flying over.

"A monster! We were walking out of the park and it attacked us!" Snips said in a rush.

"It was huge, with claws!" Snails nodded. "And big teeth!"

"A monster? I'm not surprised," Diamond Tiara said loudly. "*She* probably invited it." Diamond Tiara pointed a hoof at Lilymoon. The ponies all turned to look at Lilymoon, who glared back at them.

"It wasn't me!" she said defiantly.

Apple Bloom agreed fiercely. "Yeah! She's been with us the whole time!" The CMCs nodded. Zipporwhill's father stepped forward to speak to Snips and Snails.

"Are you sure you did not just encounter the characters I hired for the party?" he asked, gesturing to several ponies in large puppy and kitty costumes. Snips and Snails shook their heads, looking back at the park entrance.

"No, because they're over there...and the monster is *right there*!"

Sweetie Belle whirled to see that the colts were right. A hulking, dark form stood in the shadows at the park's entrance. It tilted back its fierce head and howled.

"It's a Timberwolf!" Lilymoon shouted.

The Timberwolf charged into the party.

CHAPTER FIVE

Sweetie Belle was frozen in fear as the
Timberwolf bounded into the park. Its
glowing green eyes burned in the darkness.
A putrid stench of earth and rotting logs
poured from its mouth with every rasping
breath. Its "fur" was made of leaves, and
its four legs and body were covered in
bark, like a living tree-creature. Snips and
Snails were right—it had giant teeth and
claws. The birthday party exploded into
chaos. Ponies screamed and stampeded out
of the park as the beast stalked forward,
growling. Zipporwhill's father scooped up
his struggling daughter in his hooves and
flapped his wings skyward.

"My puppy!" Zipporwhill reached her

hooves toward a small brown dog across the park. The little Pegasus squirmed free of her father's grip and flew to grab her puppy. He licked her muzzle in thanks, then began to bark ferociously at something behind Zipporwhill. She turned slowly, her eyes widening in fear. The monster was stalking toward her, head low, jaws agape.

Sweetie Belle gasped as the creature gave a guttural growl and leaped at the birthday pony. Zipporwhill screamed and ducked, flying under the beast, her tiara skimming its belly. The Timberwolf's fangs sank into the piñata dangling behind her, and it shook it vigorously like a dog. As the papier-mâché ripped, sugary missiles of candy flew everywhere.

"Hide!" Lilymoon said as she shoved

the Cutie Mark Crusaders under the cake cart and dashed into the fray.

Sweetie Belle peeked out from the tablecloth and watched as the Timberwolf bounded atop the table of candy. It threw its head back, devouring the sweets with huge gulps. Once it was finished, it raised its muzzle and sniffed the air. Then, it whipped its head toward the cupcake-decorating station. "Oh no," Sweetie Belle whispered. Diamond Tiara and Silver Spoon were trapped inside the cupcake booth, huddled together in terror.

"Run!" the Cutie Mark Crusaders yelled. But either the ponies didn't hear them or they were too afraid to do anything. The Timberwolf took a flying leap from the now-empty candy table and loped toward the cupcake booth. Diamond Tiara and Silver Spoon

whimpered as the monster approached, sharp wooden teeth gnashing the air.

Suddenly, a cupcake flew from the station and splattered on the Timberwolf's snout. Then another and another! It licked the frosting off its nose and turned to see who its attacker was. Sweetie Belle couldn't believe it! Lilymoon was facing off against the beast, using her magic to hurl cupcakes as fast as she could.

"Run!" Lilymoon called to Diamond Tiara and Silver Spoon. "I'll hold it off!" The terrified ponies didn't need to be told twice. They cantered away to safety.

"She's running out of cupcakes!" Scootaloo hissed.

"We gotta help her!" Apple Bloom said.

Sweetie Belle gulped as her two friends stuck their heads out from under the cake cart and yelled with all their might: *"HEY, TIMBERWOLF! OVER HERE!"*

The beast whipped its head toward the noise, green eyes ablaze. In two huge leaps, it reached the cake cart. Scootaloo and Apple Bloom quickly ducked back under the tablecloth. Sweetie Belle whimpered as she heard the Timberwolf circle the cart. The CMCs held their breaths.

"It's standing next to us," Scootaloo breathed, eyes wide. Sweetie Belle shuddered as she heard the Timberwolf devour the cake above them in loud, messy bites. Then suddenly, the creature stopped eating.

"Is it gone?" Apple Bloom asked.

With a snuffle, the creature stuck its wooden snout under the tablecloth! The Cutie Mark Crusaders screamed and dove away from it.

Then, a blast of Unicorn magic wrapped a ribbon around the Timberwolf's muzzle, tying a bow. Sweetie Belle looked over to see Rarity galloping to the rescue. Applejack raced in to stand protectively in front of the Crusaders. As the Timberwolf pawed at the bow entangling its jaws, Fluttershy stepped forward to address the beast.

"Excuse me, but you were *not* invited to this party. I think you had better go back to the Everfree Forest where you belong!" Fluttershy said sternly.

"Or we're gonna *make* ya go back," Applejack added fiercely. The Timberwolf growled, but to Sweetie Belle's relief, it turned tail and raced out of the park.

"Are y'all all right?" Applejack asked with concern. Rarity dashed over.

"Oh, Sweetie Belle," she said, scooping

her sister into a hug. "Darling, you must have been so frightened."

"I'm *fine*!" Sweetie Belle said, annoyed that Rarity had basically called her a scaredy-pony in front of all her friends, even though she *was* relieved her sister had appeared.

"We're all okay, thanks to Lilymoon!" Apple Bloom said, nodding toward the young Unicorn. Lilymoon was looking around the party.

"Where's my sister?" she asked. But just then, Ambermoon came rushing over from some nearby booths.

"Let's *go*, Lilymoon," she snapped without so much as looking at anypony else. Lilymoon shrugged to the others and rushed off to join her sour-faced sister.

"Y'all should be gettin' home, too,"

Applejack said. "Rarity, ya mind walkin' 'em back?"

"I'm happy to. Now, everypony, just stick close to me. I shall ensure no creature harms a hair on your manes!" Rarity said, gathering the CMCs close.

But as they left, Sweetie Belle looked back over her shoulder at the wreckage of the party. The Timberwolf had eaten the birthday cake, but oddly, it hadn't touched the bone-shaped dog cake.

"I don't understand," she heard Fluttershy tell Applejack. "Timberwolves never leave the Forest without a good reason. I wonder if it was sick."

Sweetie Belle was wondering something herself—what if that monster came back?

CHAPTER SIX

The next day in the schoolyard, everypony was talking about the Timberwolf.

"Did you see its teeth?" Featherweight asked.

"Did you smell its breath?" Peachy Pie countered.

"That was the scariest birthday party ever," said Cotton Cloudy.

Twist listened with wide eyes and sighed. "I wath tho bummed I was thick and didn't get to go, but I gueth I thould be glad I mithed it!"

Sweetie Belle, Scootaloo, and Apple Bloom hung back with Lilymoon. They did not feel like reliving last night's adventure.

"Good thing we saw that monster first

and warned you all," Snips bragged to the class. "We basically saved everypony's life."

But Diamond Tiara was having none of it. "You didn't do anything except run away." She sniffed. Then she turned to scan the playground, eyes narrowed. "Where's Lilymoon?"

"Here we go again," Scootaloo muttered. Sweetie Belle got ready to defend Lilymoon. But Diamond Tiara surprised them all.

"*She's* the real hero!" she said, smiling at Lilymoon. "She chased that horrible thing away from Silver Spoon and me."

"Probably scared it away 'cause she's so weird," Snips said. Snails laughed. Diamond Tiara whirled on the Unicorns.

"You think defending me from creepy tree-creatures is weird?" she demanded.

"We should all thank Lilymoon. We're lucky she's in our class." Diamond Tiara put her hoof around the new pony.

Lilymoon looked uncomfortable. "Apple Bloom and Scootaloo saved *me* from the Timberwolf, too," she muttered.

"What did you do?" Silver Spoon asked.

"Aw, it was nuthin'." Apple Bloom said.

"The best part was when the Timberwolf almost ate us!" Scootaloo said, cutting off her friend. The class leaned in, excited to hear what happened next. Only Sweetie Belle stood back from the group. She felt horrible. She'd just hidden under the cart and hoped she'd stay safe. Lilymoon, Apple Bloom, and Scootaloo had all been so brave.

Maybe Snips was right. Maybe she *was* a scaredy-pony.

CHAPTER SEVEN

Sweetie Belle was troubled for the rest of the day. It seemed like everypony was braver than she was. Nopony could say that she hadn't had her fair share of exciting adventures. But even her closest friends went out of their way to point out that she was the pony who always freaked out first. It was still on her mind when she went to bed that night. So when she was jolted awake by the sound of a mournful howl, she tried to convince herself it was just her overactive imagination. A second, closer howl convinced her it was real. Sweetie Belle ducked under the covers, barely breathing. She heard shouting and running hoofbeats. Something was happening outside. Something scary.

Sweetie Belle wanted to stay there, with the covers over her head, until morning. But she heard her friends' voices in her head, calling her a scaredy-pony. Very slowly, she slid out of bed and moved to the window. Taking a deep breath, she forced herself to look outside.

Rarity was cantering down the street, toward Applejack and Twilight Sparkle, who stood outside Sugarcube Corner. In the light of the full moon, Sweetie Belle could see that the sweet shop's front window had been smashed! Sweetie Belle was still scared, but her curiosity was stronger. She ran downstairs and stepped outside. She started down the street, but two shadowy figures stepped out from a nearby alley. Sweetie Belle screamed... and so did the shadows! As they stepped into the light, Sweetie Belle realized it was Apple Bloom and Scootaloo.

"Don't sneak up on us like that!" Scootaloo said.

"Me? You're the ones hiding in the dark in the middle of the night!" Sweetie Belle protested. Then she added, "Um, why are you hiding in the dark in the middle of the night?"

"The Timberwolf is back!" Apple Bloom blurted. "It attacked Sugarcube Corner!" Sweetie Belle's eyes went wide.

"But it's gone now, right?" she asked, looking around nervously.

"Yep. Mrs. Cake told Applejack what

happened, and she rounded up the others. They all headed over to investigate, so we tagged along," Apple Bloom explained.

"Why didn't you come get *me*?" Sweetie Belle frowned, feeling left out.

"We...didn't want to wake you up!" Scootaloo said. Sweetie Belle looked at her friends suspiciously.

"And...we thought you'd be scared," Scootaloo admitted.

Sweetie Belle *was* scared. But she didn't want to admit it. "I'm a Cutie Mark Crusader! Where you go, I go!" she said. Scootaloo and Apple Bloom smiled and high-hooved Sweetie Belle. Then they galloped down the street to the sweet shop. When they got there, Mrs. Cake was already telling Twilight, Applejack, and Rarity her tale, while Mr. Cake tried to rock the babies, Pumpkin and Pound, back to sleep.

"...And when I came downstairs, there was the monster, eating my éclairs! I didn't think; I just grabbed my rolling pin and chased it away!" Mrs. Cake said.

Sweetie Belle peered around the wreckage of Sugarcube Corner. Half-eaten pastries sagged in the display case, and the normally candy-packed shelves were stripped bare. Even the cake-decorating sugar sprinkles were gone. Her hoof touched something sticky, and she looked down. She had stepped on a caramel apple with massive canine bite marks in it. Sweetie Belle kicked the confection off her hoof and shuddered.

Rainbow Dash flew in, with Fluttershy a wingbeat behind. "We checked everywhere in town!" Rainbow Dash reported. "No sign of the Timberwolf. And those things are pretty hard to hide!"

"I've never heard of a lone Timberwolf attacking a shop before," Twilight said thoughtfully. "Every book I've read says they usually run in packs and prefer the deep forest."

Pinkie Pie bounded down the stairs, yawning. She stopped in her tracks when she saw the huge crowd gathered.

"What's everypony doing here?" she asked brightly. "Is it a surprise party? Who are we surprising? Is it me?" Then she put her hooves over her mouth in concern. "Did I just ruin the surprise part?" she whispered loudly. "I promise I won't tell myself!"

"No, Pinkie," Twilight said, "Sugarcube Corner was attacked by a

Timberwolf. You mean you didn't hear any of it?"

"I'm a heavy sleeper," Pinkie said with a shrug. To demonstrate, she immediately fell asleep standing up, mouth open in a loud snore.

"Pinkie Pie!" Applejack shouted. Pinkie jumped awake again.

"What's everypony doing here?" she asked, smiling brightly. "I just had the *straaaangest* dream that you were throwing me a surprise party!"

"I think we should look for clues!" Apple Bloom said, getting things back on track.

"We have to find that Timberwolf before it strikes again!" Scootaloo said.

"Yeah!" Sweetie Belle added, trying to sound like she meant it.

"You three aren't doin' anything. This

is grown-up pony business," Applejack informed the CMCs. "You listenin', Apple Bloom?" she added for good measure.

"Yes," Apple Bloom said sulkily. "But we'd be a big help—"

"I know you would, sugarcube," said Applejack, smiling at her little sister fondly. "But the best thing you can do for us right now is stay safe."

Sweetie Belle gave the tiniest sigh of relief. Staying safe was *definitely* something she could do.

"Actually," said Twilight, "I think I *do* have a job for you three." Apple Bloom and Scootaloo brightened. Sweetie Belle winced. "You can help Mr. and Mrs. Cake clean up their shop!"

Apple Bloom and Scootaloo sagged. Sweetie Belle beamed.

"Meanwhile, the rest of us will try
to find that Timberwolf and stop it
from attacking again. Maybe Starlight
Glimmer and I can find a spell to help."
Twilight trotted off to find Starlight.

As Sweetie Belle looked at the fang
marks in the caramel apple, she was
glad to leave the Timberwolf hunting to
Twilight. Still, she felt like maybe she was
noticing a pattern to the monster's attacks.
And if she was right...she was giving up
sugar forever.

CHAPTER EIGHT

"This meeting of the Cutie Mark Crusaders has been called to try 'n' figure out what that Timberwolf is up to!" Apple Bloom announced.

Lilymoon looked from Apple Bloom to Scootaloo and Sweetie Belle. "Does it matter that I'm not a Cutie Mark Crusader?" she asked.

They shook their heads. With all the craziness going on (which they were specifically told *not* to get involved in), Apple Bloom suggested they meet at the Crusaders Clubhouse. At the very least they could try to come up with some ideas to help out their sisters and the others.

"First item on the list," Apple Bloom

read from her notes, "what makes Timberwolves attack?"

"Somepony insulted them?" Scootaloo suggested.

"Their forest home was destroyed?" Lilymoon offered.

"Their bark is worse than their bite?" Scootaloo said, grinning.

"Revenge?" Lilymoon asked.

"Good! What else?" Apple Bloom jotted notes down on a big piece of paper. Sweetie Belle had an idea, but it sounded pretty crazy, even to her . . . and she was the one who had thought of it! Apple Bloom turned to look at her. "You haven't said anythin' yet, Sweetie Belle. Don'tcha have any ideas?" Sweetie Belle took a deep breath, then launched into her theory in a rush.

"I think the Timberwolf isn't attacking ponies. It's going after sugar! Like at Zipporwhill's birthday party: It ate all the candy on the table. And it went after cupcakes. And it ate the birthday cake, which was sweet, but not the dog cake, which wasn't! And then, it attacked the sugariest part of Ponyville, Mrs. Cake's shop. But it didn't touch anything but the candy and sweets!" Sweetie Belle stopped talking. The others stared at her.

Finally, Apple Bloom sighed. "If you don't have a serious suggestion, you don't need to make stuff up," she said.

"But I *am* being serious!" Sweetie Belle said, her voice cracking indignantly.

"Who ever heard of a Timberwolf eating candy? That's not what those big teeth are for," Scootaloo said.

"Actually," Lilymoon said thoughtfully, "Sweetie Belle might be onto something."

"What?" Scootaloo blurted.

"Ha!" Sweetie Belle said.

"Have you ever heard of wereponies?" Lilymoon asked the others. "Ponies who change into different creatures?"

"There was that one time Fluttershy turned into a vampire fruit bat-pony..." Apple Bloom said, remembering.

"Like that." Lilymoon nodded. "Only it happens on a full moon."

"You think the Timberwolf may be actually...a pony?" Scootaloo asked, her eyes wide.

"Which pony?" Sweetie Belle asked nervously. She knew it couldn't be her friends or her sister, since they had all been around when the monster showed up. But what if it was somepony else she knew, like Mayor Mare? Or Miss Cheerilee!

"I don't know." Lilymoon shrugged. "I'm just saying, this Timberwolf isn't acting like a real Timberwolf. Especially when it comes to candy. But if it was really a werepony who had a sweet tooth..."

"Well, how do you spot a werepony?" Apple Bloom asked.

"I don't know," Lilymoon admitted again. "But I know where we can find out!"

CHAPTER NINE

"I'm *sure* there's a chapter on wereponies in *The Lost Creatures of Equestria*," Lilymoon said as they walked up Horseshoe Hill.

"Didn't we tell our sisters we weren't gonna get into any more monster trouble?" Sweetie Belle asked.

"We aren't gettin' into trouble," Apple Bloom said. "We're just gatherin' information."

Sweetie Belle had a feeling "gathering information" would quickly turn into "getting into trouble." But she didn't want them to think she was scared, so she let it go.

As they reached Lilymoon's house, the front door flew open, and Ambermoon came trotting out. She saw them and rolled her eyes. "Don't you three have your *own* homes to go to?" she asked.

"Sure. But if we didn't come visit, nopony would be around to tell you that you'd be a lot happier if you weren't so nasty all the time," Scootaloo shot back. Ambermoon's eyes widened in surprise.

"Where are you going?" Lilymoon asked quickly, changing the subject.

Ambermoon continued glaring at Scootaloo but answered her sister's question. "Well, since *somepony* in this house keeps stealing my candy, I'm going into town to get some more."

"*Ugh!*" Lilymoon groaned. "I'll never borrow *anything* from you *ever* again, happy?"

"Happi*er*," Ambermoon said as she trotted down the hill.

"So?" Apple Bloom asked casually. "Has your sister *always* liked candy?"

"Yeah...she's had a sweet tooth for as long as I can..." Lilymoon's eyes widened. "But...it couldn't be her! She was at the party with us!"

"She *did* kinda disappear right before the Timberwolf showed up, though," Apple Bloom pointed out.

"And you *did* say she acts weirder during a full moon," Sweetie Belle reminded her.

"I *totally* bet it's her!" Scootaloo said. "*That's* why she's so mean."

"She's *always* that mean." Lilymoon shrugged. "It doesn't mean she's a werepony."

"Wereponies?" Somepony cackled above them. They all looked up to see

Auntie Eclipse trotting down the stairs. "Now, why would such innocent little fillies be talking about wereponies?"

Sweetie Belle glanced nervously at the others. Should they tell Auntie Eclipse what they thought was going on? Lilymoon subtly shook her head. Sweetie Belle sighed. Of course they weren't gonna do that.

"We just...uh...have a report for class," Apple Bloom lied.

"Everypony got different creatures," Scootaloo added. "We got a werepony! So we were just gonna check out a book in your library to see what it said about ponies and Timberwolves and—"

"Timberwolves?" Auntie Eclipse interrupted her. "You want to know about ponies turning into Timberwolves!" The ponies nodded. "Timberwolves aren't like regular wolves."

"Duh," Scootaloo said. "They're made of timber." Auntie Eclipse arched an eyebrow at Scootaloo. "Sorry," she said quickly.

"It's a rare magic that brings wood to life. In fact, it's only ever been found in one place in all of Equestria."

"The Everfree Forest?" Lilymoon asked.

Auntie Eclipse nodded. "Timberwolves have never been spotted anywhere else. And you won't find any books about ponies turning into Timberwolves because it's not possible. Not the same way they would turn into a werepony. Seems like a strange assignment to give young fillies...." Auntie Eclipse let the comment hang in the air. The young ponies all glanced at one another, unsure of what to say next.

"Thanks for your help," Apple Bloom finally said. "I'm sure we can find the rest of what we need on our own." She started toward the library.

"Actually," Auntie Eclipse said, stepping in front of her, "I'll be needing the library this afternoon. I'm sure you have more than enough information...for a school project." She strode into the library, the door magically closing behind her.

"Wow," Scootaloo said. "Guess she really doesn't want us in there."

"Great," Lilymoon said. "Where are we gonna get answers now?"

"*Actually*," Apple Bloom said with a grin, "there may be *some*pony who could help us...."

CHAPTER TEN

Sweetie Belle shuddered at the spooky trees and strange sounds of creatures that stayed *just* out of sight. For somepony who didn't like scary places, she sure found herself in the Everfree Forest a whole lot. Fortunately, she knew where they were going, and that place didn't scare her at all . . . anymore. Still, Sweetie Belle didn't want to spend any more time in the spooky forest than she absolutely had to.

"You know a Zebra? And she lives *in* the Everfree Forest?" Lilymoon asked as they walked along the path. "You think she'll help us?"

"Zecora helped me when I got Cutie Pox," Apple Bloom said. "I betcha she knows about curing other curses, too." They turned a corner and saw a hooded figure gathering plants just off the path. The figure turned and regarded the fillies.

"Four ponies where there are usually three—have you all come out here just to see me?" The figure removed her hood, and Zecora smiled at them.

"Hi, Zecora!" the Crusaders said in unison.

Zecora glanced at Lilymoon. "I'm always happy to have guests. Who might you be? I know the rest."

"H-hi," Lilymoon said shyly, "I'm Lilymoon. My family just moved here."

Zecora nodded, then turned and walked along the path. "Follow me and sit a spell. I'm sure you all have much to tell," she said over her shoulder. The others quickly followed.

Sweetie Belle heard Lilymoon gasp when they arrived at Zecora's home. It *was* pretty impressive. Zecora lived inside a giant tree. Different-colored bottles filled with Celestia-knew-what dangled from the branches outside. Sweetie Belle looked around as they walked through the door. A cauldron was bubbling, odd objects hung on the walls, and the shelves were filled with spells and potions. Zecora checked the bubbling cauldron as she regarded the young ponies.

"I sense this is more than a friendly visit? You all look worried; so come now, what is it?"

"We know it sounds crazy, but we

think the Timberwolf that attacked Ponyville is really a werepony," Apple Bloom explained.

Zecora's eyes widened. "A werepony can bring much danger. But a werepony Timberwolf? That's even stranger."

"Very strange," Lilymoon agreed. "My aunt told us a werepony Timberwolf was impossible."

"I don't want to say that your aunt was wrong, but it *is* possible, if the magic is strong." Lilymoon looked surprised that her aunt might not be right about something. Zecora cocked her head. "But I'm confused. Please explain to me: Why would a Timberwolf be a pony?"

Scootaloo nodded to Sweetie Belle, who was getting way more comfortable in Zecora's familiar home than out in the Forest. "I noticed that both times this Timberwolf attacked, it only ate candy," Sweetie Belle said. "Which seemed really weird."

"Yes, I see," said Zecora, "that is quite suspicious. You think it's somepony who finds candy delicious." The ponies nodded. "A spell this strong is very impressive. But the pony who cast it is clearly aggressive."

"I didn't even think about that," Apple Bloom admitted. "Who would turn a pony into a Timberwolf?"

"*Why* would someone turn a pony into a Timberwolf?" Scootaloo added.

Zecora looked away from the ponies. She stared out the window into the Forest beyond. Sweetie Belle thought she looked...worried? "I have an idea, but I don't want to say. I believe that's a tale to tell some other day. For now, let's just focus on getting a cure. We will know more when it's time, I am sure."

Zecora wandered around the room as she spoke, gathering bottles, herbs, and various ingredients. She tossed them into the boiling cauldron. "To avoid serious trouble, there is no time to waste. You must locate the pony and do it with haste!"

"You mean so it won't have time to attack again?" asked Scootaloo.

Zecora shook her head. "There are bigger things at play than you understand. If you don't cure this pony as fast as you can, it may never turn back to a pony again!" The fillies all looked at one another.

"It becomes permanent?" Sweetie Belle squeaked. Zecora nodded.

"But how are we going to figure out who it is?" Lilymoon asked.

"Maybe we already have," Scootaloo said.

"It's *not* my sister," Lilymoon insisted.

Zecora took an empty bottle and filled it with the milky-gray potion bubbling in her cauldron. "A Timberwolf pony could hide anywhere. But when you do find it, you must pluck a hair."

"We have to *what?*" Sweetie Belle asked.

Zecora handed Apple Bloom the bottle filled with potion. "Put the hair in the potion and watch it turn pink; when the pony turns Timberwolf, give it this drink."

"Are we sure we want to do this?" Sweetie Belle hesitated.

But Apple Bloom's enthusiasm overpowered the sentiment. "Wow. Thanks,

Zecora! I knew you'd know what to do!"
she said, studying the potion. She turned to
the others. "Come on, y'all! We got no time
to waste!"

The ponies all rushed toward the door—
Sweetie Belle with less speed than the
others—but Zecora's voice stopped them:
"One final thing: When the suspect you find,
here is a warning to keep in your mind." The
ponies all stopped and turned. Zecora looked
at them with a very serious expression.
"Don't let it scratch you, whatever you do, or
else you will turn into a Timberwolf, too!"

CHAPTER ELEVEN

"Did you hear her? *We* could become Timberwolves!" Sweetie Belle called, rushing after the others as they hurried toward Ponyville. Apple Bloom, Scootaloo, and Lilymoon were busy discussing what to do next.

"How do we get the Timberwolf to drink the potion?" Scootaloo asked.

"We know it likes candy. We could pour it on something sweet!" Lilymoon suggested.

Sweetie Belle couldn't believe what she was hearing. "We aren't gonna do anything!" she said loudly. Everypony turned to look at her. "Our sisters *told* us not to get into trouble, remember?" The others stopped running and considered what she said.

Apple Bloom sighed heavily. "Sweetie Belle is right, y'all," she said. "We *did* promise not to get into more mischief."

"Thank you!" Sweetie Belle was relieved.

"But everypony still thinks it's a regular Timberwolf!" Scootaloo said. "We need to tell them it's really Ambermoon!"

"We don't *know* my sister is a werepony!" Lilymoon reminded them. She thought for a minute, then: "It could be one of your sisters' friends."

"What? Who?" Apple Bloom asked.

"The pink one. Pinkie Pie? She was acting pretty strange at the party," Lilymoon pointed out.

"Yeah, but that's Pinkie. She *always* acts weird," Apple Bloom said.

"She *did* say she slept through the whole Timberwolf attack," Sweetie Belle realized. "That does seem a little suspicious."

"You just don't want Ambermoon to be the werepony, so you're trying to make us think it's Pinkie!" Scootaloo accused Lilymoon. The Unicorn rolled her eyes.

"You just don't like my sister, so you want her to be a werepony," she huffed.

Scootaloo considered that. "Okay, that's actually kind of true," she admitted.

"If we tell Rarity and her friends what we know," Sweetie Belle said, "they can check out Pinkie *and* Ambermoon."

"We should get a hair from Ambermoon's mane or tail," Apple Bloom said. "Just in case."

"Actually…" Lilymoon reached into her bag and pulled out a manebrush. "The hair

is no problem. I still haven't returned this."
She magically pulled a long black hair from
the brush. She looked at the others. "If my
sister *is* the werepony, we can handle it."

"And if it's Pinkie . . . either way, we
gotta tell the others right now!" Apple
Bloom decided. "Let's hustle, y'all!"

They raced back to Ponyville. The
sun was setting when they arrived, but
the town was bustling. They quickly
realized why. Rarity, Applejack, and
their friends were preparing to head off
into the Everfree Forest to hunt down the
Timberwolf! The CMCs had arrived just
in time! They rushed through the crowd.

"Rarity!" Sweetie Belle called. Rarity
turned and saw the fillies approaching.

"Sweetie Belle, darling, we're just a teensy
bit busy at the moment," Rarity explained.

"Perhaps whatever it is can wait until after we've dealt with this beastly business?"

"We're here because of the beastly business!" Apple Bloom explained.

"Oh *no*, you ain't," Applejack said, walking over to them. "If I told you once, I told you a dozen times: *We* are handlin' this!"

"We *know!*" Apple Bloom said. "But we need to tell you *what* you're handling!"

"Don't worry," Fluttershy said sweetly as she walked past them. "We know just how to take care of the poor creature."

"You do?" Scootaloo asked.

"Sure," Applejack said. "We're gonna find it, catch it, and take it far away where it can't harm nopony."

"You can't!" Sweetie Belle squeaked. "It's not a regular Timberwolf! It's a—"

"We doin' this or what?" Rainbow Dash called out to the others.

"One second!" Applejack called back, then turned to the fillies. "We appreciate y'all wantin' to help. But we do this stuff all the time."

"Don't worry about us," Rarity said to Sweetie Belle reassuringly.

"Rarity. We aren't worried. But you don't—"

"Pinkie, dear, are you quite all right?" asked Rarity, cutting off her sister. Sweetie Belle and the others turned and saw Pinkie Pie walking toward them, strangely subdued.

"Never better," Pinkie said. She really didn't look so good, but she was putting on a brave face for the task at hand. "Let's do this thing!" She walked past the fillies as she struggled to smile. As she passed, Sweetie Belle saw Lilymoon use magic to pluck a hair from Pinkie's tail. Nopony else noticed, and Pinkie didn't even flinch! As they trotted off, Applejack and Rarity glanced back at the fillies.

"Y'all go home. Stay outta trouble," Applejack warned.

"Don't be scared, Sweetie Belle. We shall be fine!" Rarity called. The grown-up ponies all hurried into the Forest, Twilight leading the way.

"I can't believe it," Scootaloo said.

"They wouldn't even listen to us!" Apple Bloom said, kicking her hoof in the dirt angrily. "If we're right, they're gonna take some poor pony and dump it Celestia-knows-where!"

"If it is my sister...she'll be stuck as a

Timberwolf forever." Lilymoon looked horrified.

"And if it *is* Pinkie," Scootaloo said, looking at the rising dusk, "and she transforms into a werepony when she's with the others…" They all looked up at the sky. The full moon would be out soon. Sweetie Belle was the one who finally said what they were all thinking, even though she didn't want to.

"We have to go find the Timberwolf first, don't we?"

CHAPTER TWELVE

"Are we sure this is the best plan?"
Sweetie Belle asked as she walked over
to the others. They were standing by
the entrance to the Everfree Forest. She
adjusted the knapsack on her back. They
each wore one filled with candy. They had
raided their emergency Nightmare Night
supplies to make sure they had enough for
the mission.

"We don't have a choice. We only got
one shot at this," Apple Bloom said. She
pulled Zecora's potion out of her bag. "We
go in, find the Timberwolf, and get it to
drink this here potion!"

"Well, first, we have to figure out who
the Timberwolf is," Lilymoon reminded

them. She opened her bag, one black hair and one pink hair visible inside. "Once we find out which one it is, we drop the hair in the potion…"

"And wait for it to turn pink," Scootaloo finished. She reached into her bag and pulled out a buckball-size peppermint. "Once it does, we pour the potion on this. We know that whoever it is likes candy. *This* they won't be able to pass up!"

Sweetie Belle was terrified, but she was determined to do what needed to be done. A pony's life was at stake! Maybe Ambermoon, maybe Pinkie Pie. She would *not* be a scaredy-pony.

"You ready?" Apple Bloom asked. Sweetie Belle screamed and jumped.

"Yes. Sorry. I–I'm just a little nervous,"

Sweetie Belle replied. The others looked at one another.

"Sweetie Belle, nopony will be upset if you don't come," Apple Bloom said gently.

Sweetie Belle took a deep breath. She could do this. "We have a pony to save! Let's go, Crusaders."

Apple Bloom smiled. They all hoof-bumped and marched into the Everfree Forest as the last rays of sunlight faded on the horizon.

Continuing deeper into the Forest, they left a trail of candy behind them. Whoever the Timberwolf was, the sugar would be too much to resist. After they had been at it a while, Sweetie Belle was starting to wonder if the plan was going to work at all.

Then she heard a noise.

"What was that?" Sweetie Belle asked nervously. The others stopped and listened, but there was nothing but the sounds of the Forest.

"It's just your imagination," Scootaloo said. But a second later, it happened again. This time Lilymoon heard it, too.

"It sounds like...paper?" Lilymoon said. The ponies all quietly made their way through the Forest, following the noise. Above them, clouds blanketed the night sky, blocking the moonlight and making it hard to see. However, they could *hear* the rustling noise getting louder. Scootaloo motioned to the others and pointed toward a ravine up ahead. The fillies all crept closer. They poked their heads over a ridge and looked down to see what was making the noise. A shadowy figure was hunched over a large mound of something.

"Is that… *Twist*?" Sweetie Belle whispered. Below them in the ravine, Twist sat next to a pile of candy. The rustling they had heard was her unwrapping the candy before she popped in into her mouth.

"She took all our candy!" Scootaloo said. "Now the werepony will never get it!"

"Twist! Cut it out!" Apple Bloom yelled, jumping over the ridge. Twist looked up, shocked to see them.

"What are you guyth doing out here?!" she asked nervously.

"We are *tryin'* to find a werepony. But you're eatin' all our bait!" Apple Bloom shouted.

Twist looked scared. But why would she be scared of them?

"Pleath! You all have to go!" Twist said. "Before ith too late!"

"Too late for what?" Scootaloo asked. Above them, the clouds parted, and the light of the full moon shone down on the ravine. Twist doubled over, like she had a really bad stomachache.

"You guys..." Lilymoon said, backing away slowly. Tiny leaves popped out of Twist's mane. Vines wrapped around her hooves.

"Oh no..." Scootaloo said.

"Hey. It's okay, Twist," Apple Bloom said slowly as she motioned for them all to back out of the ravine. "Why don't you keep the candy?"

Twist howled up at the moon. The fillies turned and rushed out of the ravine.

But Lilymoon suddenly stopped. She looked back at Twist.

"Hang on!" she called. She rushed down as Twist continued her transformation.

"Lilymoon! Be careful!" Sweetie Belle yelled.

Lilymoon leaped down next to Twist. Leaves, wood, and moss covered her body, but her orange tail was still visible. Lilymoon snagged a single hair in her teeth and rushed back to join the others. As they hurried out of the ravine, Sweetie Belle glanced back down. The transformation was complete.

They had found the werepony. Twist was the Timberwolf!

CHAPTER THIRTEEN

The Timberwolf snarled and stuck her wooden muzzle to snuffle at the pile of empty wrappers. There was no candy left. She sniffed the air. Her head turned, and her glowing eyes stared right at the ponies. Sweetie Belle couldn't move. Glancing to either side, she could see that for once, she wasn't the only one frozen with fear. Next to her, Scootaloo, Apple Bloom, and Lilymoon stood just as still.

Twist growled and took a few steps toward them.

"The candy. In the bags," Lilymoon whispered.

"Should we leave the candy and run?" Scootaloo asked.

"We need to get the potion ready," Apple Bloom whispered back.

"We need to get away!" Sweetie Belle said. "We can't help Twist if we're Timberwolf chow."

"I thought you said this Timberwolf only ate sweets," Scootaloo whispered.

"*You* wanna be the one to test that?" Sweetie Belle hissed.

Below them, the Timberwolf moved cautiously but steadily closer.

"Here." Lilymoon's horn glowed brightly, and the hair from Twist's tail floated over to Sweetie Belle. "You go get the potion ready while the Timberwolf is distracted."

Lilymoon charged down the ravine toward the Timberwolf. Her horn glowed, and the knapsack on her back flew into the air, just in front of Twist's wooden nose.

"Hungry?" Lilymoon shouted. Twist growled at Lilymoon but didn't take her eyes off the floating bag of candy. She swiped at it with a massive paw.

"Wow. Lilymoon is awesome," Apple Bloom said breathlessly.

"Yeah. That's brave right there," Scootaloo agreed. Sweetie Belle nodded. She could never do anything like that.

Lilymoon yelled up at them. "This is going to be a pretty lame diversion if there's nothing to *divert from*!"

"Oh. Right!" Apple Bloom grabbed the potion and pulled out the stopper. Sweetie Belle's horn glowed, and Twist's hair floated into the liquid. The Crusaders watched as the liquid began to bubble and swirl from milky gray to bright pink.

"*Oooh*. Pretty," Sweetie Belle whispered. The other two stared at her. "What?" she said. "It *is!*"

Scootaloo dug the giant peppermint out of her bag and poured the pink potion over it. The elixir soaked into the candy, and it glowed brightly.

"Um. *Hey, guys!*" Lilymoon called after them. They turned and saw her up in the branches of a tree on the opposite ridge of the ravine. Twist clawed the tree with her front paws.

"Okay, Crusaders. Let's do this!" Apple Bloom and Scootaloo rushed down the ravine. As scared as she was, Sweetie Belle was just behind them.

"Don't let her scratch you!" she reminded her friends.

The Timberwolf turned when she heard them rushing toward her.

"*Mmm,*" Scootaloo said, holding the glowing peppermint in front of her. "Doesn't this look nice and tasty, Twist?" The Timberwolf licked the bark around her mouth with her leafy tongue. She took a few steps toward them. Sweetie Belle smiled—it was going to work! They were going to save Twist!

Suddenly, a rope lassoed the Timberwolf's mouth shut and pulled her away from the peppermint! Sweetie Belle looked at the top of the ridge and saw Applejack, Rarity, and the others. Applejack held the rope and glared down at the fillies.

"Y'all step *away* from that Timberwolf."

CHAPTER FOURTEEN

"Wait!" Sweetie Belle squeaked, but nopony was listening. Twilight Sparkle blasted a beam of purple light from her horn, encasing the entire ravine in a magical shield.

"Ravine is secure," she called to the others. "Now let's get that Timberwolf and transport it out of here."

"You can't do that!" Lilymoon called from the tree.

"Oh, we can, and we totally will," Rainbow Dash said confidently as she hovered in the air. The Timberwolf leaped and tried to claw at Rainbow Dash, but Applejack tugged on the rope, jerking away the Timberwolf's muzzle.

Applejack ignored its growls and glared at her sister.

"Y'all got some serious explaining to do!" she said.

"We *will* explain, if y'all will just stop and listen for a second!" Apple Bloom replied. Rarity and Pinkie Pie slid down into the ravine and blocked the Timberwolf on either side.

"*After* you fillies are out of danger," Rarity said firmly as Fluttershy cautiously approached the Timberwolf.

"Hello there. You must be scared. How about you let us help you?" she said sweetly. The Timberwolf tried backing away from Fluttershy, but Applejack held her securely with the rope.

"Just let us feed her this peppermint,

and *then* it will all make sense!" demanded Scootaloo.

"Timberwolves don't eat peppermints, silly!" Pinkie Pie said, giggling.

"*This* one does!" Lilymoon said, leaping in front of Fluttershy. "Show them," she said to Scootaloo, using her magic to untie Applejack's lasso.

"Hey now! Stop that!" demanded Applejack. As soon as the Timberwolf was freed, she roared and tried to run away. But Twilight's shield prevented her from going anywhere.

"Here!" Scootaloo shouted as she rushed toward the Timberwolf with the peppermint.

"Whoa, whoa, whoa! What are you thinking?" Rainbow Dash said as she swooped down and grabbed Scootaloo. "That thing is dangerous!"

"No!" Scootaloo shouted as the peppermint flew out of her hooves and landed in the dirt below, right next to Sweetie Belle, who picked it up.

"Toss it here, Sweetie Belle!" Apple Bloom called.

"Sweetie Belle, you put that down this instant!" Rarity shouted.

The Timberwolf crouched defensively, her back against Twilight's shield.

"Oh for Cerberus's sake," Lilymoon said, running toward Sweetie Belle and the peppermint, "none of you are listening! Sweetie Belle, throw it to me!"

Pinkie bounced over and hugged Lilymoon tightly, then asked, "Hey, what gives, sister? Are you on Team Pony or Team Timberwolf here?"

The Timberwolf was ready to leap at anypony who came close. Applejack rushed toward it. The Timberwolf slashed at her with her claws. Sweetie Belle gasped! At the last moment, Applejack ducked, and the wooden claws harmlessly raked against her hat.

"A little scratch ain't gonna bother me none, fella," Applejack said, looking for an opening.

"*Sis!*" Apple Bloom ran and barreled into her older sister, knocking her out of the way just as the Timberwolf slashed at her again. "Stay back! If she scratches you, you'll turn into a Timberwolf, too!"

"Say what, now?" Applejack asked as she stood up.

"Twist is a werepony," Lilymoon explained.

"Twist? That's *Twist*?" Pinkie Pie asked.

"That's what we've been *trying to tell you!*" Scootaloo called from above, still in Rainbow Dash's hooves. Everypony started talking at once.

The Timberwolf turned in a snarling circle, confused by all the shouting. Sweetie Belle stared at the peppermint in her hooves. Looking around, she saw that everypony was busy yelling. She really wished she could explain it all and not have to be the brave one, but so far that had been a disaster. This *had* to be done—now. Sweetie Belle took a big breath. She didn't think about it. She just ran as fast as she could toward Twist.

"Sweetie Belle! No!" Rarity called. But Sweetie Belle kept going. The Timberwolf turned toward her and roared out a fog of sour green breath.

"Not a scaredy-pony. Not a scaredy-pony. Not a scaredy-pony," Sweetie Belle whispered to herself over and over again. Just a few more feet. She was almost there. Everypony shouted as Sweetie Belle jumped into the air. The Timberwolf leaped to meet her, its jaws gaping wide... and Sweetie Belle jammed the peppermint into the Timberwolf's wide mouth.

CHAPTER FIFTEEN

The Timberwolf collapsed, as if she had suddenly fallen into a deep sleep. Rarity rushed toward Sweetie Belle and helped her up.

"Sweetie Belle, what were you thinking?" she asked.

"Somepony had to help Twist," Sweetie Belle said shakily. Twilight's shield vanished, and she trotted over to join them.

"Now, what is all this about a werepony?" Twilight asked.

"It's a long story," Lilymoon stated. "But the short version is, Sweetie Belle figured out the Timberwolf was a werepony, we got a cure from Zecora, and then—"

"We *tried* to tell y'all so you could handle it. But you were so busy protectin' us, you wouldn't listen," Apple Bloom finished, glaring at her sister.

"So we had to deal with it ourselves," Scootaloo explained. "We thought the Timberwolf was either Lilymoon's sister or Pinkie Pie."

"Why me?" Pinkie Pie asked, shocked.

"You were acting really weird at Zipporwhill's party," Apple Bloom said, "and you said you slept through the Timberwolf attack on Sugarcube Corner."

"*Ohhhhhh.* Well, that's because I was trying to break the Equestria record for Earth pony unicycle juggling on the first night of a full moon. See?" Pinkie whipped three unicycles out of nowhere and began juggling them as the others gaped. "It made me kinda tired the next day."

"Anyhow...we came out here because we were worried about you guys," Scootaloo continued. "And then we found out the Timberwolf was Twist. But we couldn't let you send her away, or she'd get stuck as a werepony forever!"

"Wow," Twilight said. "That's...really good work."

"Definitely," Rainbow Dash added. "You guys were pretty awesome. *Especially* standing up to us!"

"Hey now," Applejack said as Rarity sniffed. "Don't push it."

Behind them, somepony groaned. A pile of wood, leaves, and bark lay where the Timberwolf had been. Twist poked out her head. She looked around, confused.

"Hey, you guyth. Whath goin' on?" she asked. Lilymoon and the Crusaders rushed over to her.

"Twist, are you okay?" Sweetie Belle asked.

"I think tho," she responded.

"What happened?" asked Apple Bloom.

"I hafth *no* idea," Twist said as she crawled out of the pile. "I got home from thchool the other day and felt groth. Tho I thtayed home from the party. But then... I had a crathy dream...and I wanted to eat loth and loth of candy...I thaw thom ponies in the Forest, and felt really funny..."

"It wasn't a dream," Lilymoon said seriously. Then she smiled and nodded toward Apple Bloom, Scootaloo, and Sweetie Belle. "But you're okay now. Thanks to the Cutie Mark Crusaders."

Apple Bloom put her hoof around Lilymoon and said, "*All* the Cutie Mark Crusaders." Lilymoon beamed.

"I guess I owe you an apology, sugarcube," Applejack told her sister. "We shoulda listened to y'all."

"It's okay...for *now*." Apple Bloom smiled. "But *next* time you'd better listen."

"Next time? I swear, you just love findin' trouble, don'tcha?"

As the Apple sisters continued to bicker, Rarity turned to Sweetie Belle.

"Sweetie Belle, darling, I'm so proud of you," she said.

"*Awwww*...I'm just glad I wasn't a scaredy-pony," Sweetie Belle said happily.

"Are you kidding?" Scootaloo said. "After *that* move? *Nopony* can ever call you scared again!"

Twilight was staring up at the moon thoughtfully. She looked at the Crusaders.

"Even though I don't love you putting yourselves in danger, we all owe you our thanks. You did some excellent research. But did you ever figure out *how* Twist became a werepony?" The Crusaders all shook their heads.

"That's the one thing we can't quite get," Apple Bloom admitted. Twilight looked troubled.

"What's wrong, Twilight?" Rainbow Dash asked.

"There's some dangerous magic being cast here in Ponyville. And I don't like it." The Alicorn princess frowned.

CHAPTER SIXTEEN

"And then, Sweetie Belle galloped past everypony, ran straight at the Timberwolf, *leaped* into the air"—Scootaloo jumped onto the seesaw on the playground for dramatic effect—"and soared across the ravine. The Timberwolf jumped up at her, her sharp claws slashing the air! *Wshh!* *Wshh!* But Sweetie Belle wasn't having it! She crammed the candy *right* in the monster's slobbering jaws!" Scootaloo turned to Twist. "No offense."

"It'th fine!" Twist said, grinning. "Thath totally what happened! Thweetie Belle thaved my life!" The other ponies on the playground all turned to look at

Sweetie Belle, who was standing off to the side, blushing.

"*That* Sweetie Belle?" Snips asked.

"Are you *sure*?" Snails added.

"It wasn't exactly like that. Everypony helped." Sweetie Belle wanted her friends to get the credit they deserved.

"But you *did* leap into the air and make Twist eat the candy?" Silver Spoon confirmed.

"Um. Yeah." Sweetie Belle's blush intensified. It was nice not being the scaredy-pony anymore, but all the attention made her nervous.

"Weren't you frightened?" Pip wondered.

"How did you figure it all out?" Diamond Tiara looked very impressed.

"Lilymoon did. She's the one who

guessed the Timberwolf was really a werepony," Sweetie Belle explained. The other ponies turned and looked at Lilymoon, who smiled shyly.

"Well," Diamond Tiara announced, "between that and saving our lives at the party, I just don't know *how* we managed to survive in Ponyville without you!" The ponies gathered around Lilymoon, asking her what other cool and mysterious things she knew about. As she answered, she glanced over to the Cutie Mark Crusaders and smiled gratefully. Apple Bloom, Sweetie Belle, and Scootaloo all watched her proudly.

"Looks like Lilymoon is finally settling in," Scootaloo observed. "Guess it's a happy ending for everypony."

"*Mmm-hm!*" Sweetie Belle agreed.

"Rarity *finally* forgave me for the fabric we took for the bogle. She said next time we go monster hunting, just check with her first."

"Yeah, Applejack feels awful about almost sendin' Twist away," Apple Bloom said, grinning. "She promised to listen to us about stuff like this from now on. And you know my sister never lies."

Twist joined the Crusaders. "Thankth again, you guyth. Thorry if I thcared you when I wath a Timberwolf."

"We're just glad you're okay," Apple Bloom said.

"Well, not *totally* okay," Twist said, frowning. "The thought of thomething thweet maketh me thick now. The latht *normal* pieth of candy I ate wath that candy cane I got from Lilymoon." She ran off to join the other ponies, and Scootaloo looked at the others.

"That's the candy cane that came from Ambermoon's room! And right after eating it, Twist got so sick she had to miss Zipporwhill's party."

"Only she didn't," Apple Bloom added. "She showed up as a Timberwolf!"

"You think the candy cane turned her into a werepony?" Sweetie Belle asked. "That's crazy!"

"Well, we used a peppermint to cure her," Apple Bloom pointed out. "Is it any weirder that a candy cane started this whole thing?"

"So I was *almost* right!" Scootaloo said triumphantly. "Ambermoon wasn't the werepony, but she's the one who *turned* Twist into a werepony!"

"Maybe," Apple Bloom said, working through it in her head. "But nopony expected Twist to eat that candy. So it's not like Ambermoon did it on purpose."

"Still," Sweetie Belle wondered, "why would Ambermoon have a candy cane that could turn a pony into a Timberwolf?" They all looked over at Lilymoon, who seemed to actually be enjoying herself with the rest of the class.

"She's finally fitting in and now *this* happens?" Sweetie Belle sighed.

"Let's keep it to ourselves for now," Apple Bloom said.

"Because you don't wanna tell her that her sister is evil?" asked Scootaloo.

"No," Apple Bloom said. "I wanna wait until we know if she's in on it or not."

Although things hadn't gone exactly as The Pony had planned, the experiment had still proven useful. It seemed that a Timberwolf was difficult to control, even if there was a pony inside. Using a werepony to get past the Timberwolf guardians wasn't the way to reach the Livewood. If The Pony wanted the Artifact, another plan was needed.

But first, The Pony would have to deal with the Cutie Mark Crusaders. The Pony had gone back to study the scrolls. They were clear that the Artifact would be activated by "the matching marks three." The Pony had thought there was only one group with such marks. But apparently, that wasn't the case.

Fortunately, those meddling ponies had made a habit of coming up to the house on Horseshoe Hill. It wouldn't be a problem to arrange for a little "accident" sometime soon to make sure they didn't cause any more trouble.

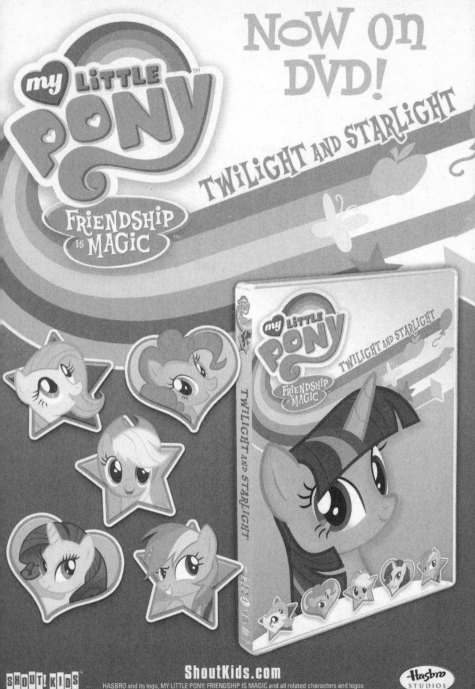